The Spider's Gift

A Ukrainian Christmas Story

retold by

Eric A. Kimmel

illustrated by

Katya Krenina

Holiday House / New York

The publisher would like to thank Mark Andryczyk, Associate
Research Scholar, Harriman Institute, Columbia University, and
Ukrainian Studies administrator at Columbia University, for
reviewing the Ukrainian words in this book for accuracy.

Library of Congress Cataloging-in-Publication Data

Kimmel, Eric A.
The spider's gift : a Ukrainian Christmas story / retold by Eric A. Kimmel ;
illustrated by Katya Krenina. — 1st ed.
p. cm.
Summary: Katrusya's family cannot afford Christmas, but they cut a small pine tree
in the forest, decorate it with buttons, and, when baby spiders hatch in its branches,
they especially enjoy the silvery webs that appear.
ISBN 978-0-8234-1743-8 (hardcover)
[1. Christmas—Folklore. 2. Spiders—Folklore. 3. Folklore—Ukraine.]
I. Krenina, Katya, ill. II. Title.
PZ8.1.K567Sp 2010
398.2'0947702—dc22
2004054162

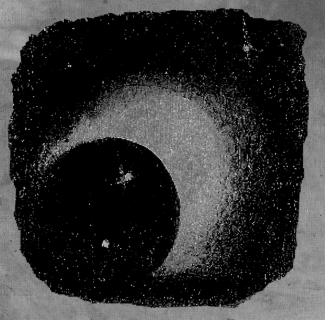

To Katya and Aliya Pauline
E. A. K.

To Eric
K. K.

"No Christmas?" Katrusya repeated the terrible words. "Did Father and Grandfather really say that?"

"It's true," her older brother Danilo answered. "I was milking the cow when I overheard them."

Katrusya carried the dripping water pails back to the house, growing angrier with every step.

"No Christmas!" she grumbled as she emptied the pails.

"No Christmas!" she muttered as she stacked the yoke and pails beside the wood pile.

"No Christmas!" she shouted as she stamped inside the house. "It isn't fair!"

Mama looked up from her spinning. Grandmother set her knitting aside. Katrusya's older sister, Anna, laid down her embroidery.

"Angry words have no place in this house," Mama said.

Katrusya scowled. "I don't care! Danilo heard Tato and Grandfather talking in the barn. He says we are to have no Christmas."

In walked Grandfather, brushing the snow from his coat. "Who's making this noise? What troop of Cossacks is camping here?"

Katrusya didn't laugh. "Danilo says there's to be no Christmas. Is it true?"

Grandfather sighed. He called Father in from the barn. Katrusya's brothers, Ivan and Danilo, came in covered with snow. The family gathered around the stove. Father spoke first.

"What Danilo and Katrusya heard is true. There will be no Christmas this year. We have no choice."

"Why, Tato?" Katrusya asked.

"We all know why," Grandfather said. "We had a poor harvest this year. We have enough food to get through the winter. But there is no money for extra things."

"Like Christmas presents," the children said.

"Does that mean we are to have no tree, too?" Katrusya asked. "We have to have a tree."

"Trees grow in the forest. It doesn't cost anything to have a tree," said her brothers.

"We can make our own presents," said Anna.

"We made our own presents when I was a little girl," Grandmother said. "But Christmas is coming in a few days. Do we have enough time?"

"We will be ready," Katrusya promised.

The next morning Katrusya and Grandfather went off to find a Christmas tree. "Which way shall we go?" Grandfather asked Katrusya.

"That way!" Katrusya said.

At last Katrusya exclaimed, "Here is our tree!" She pointed to a fir as tall as she was.

Grandfather nodded. "It's a pretty tree. I can't see how it is different from the others."

"It's special! I can feel it," Katrusya said.

Grandfather cut down the tree with three strokes from his hatchet. He and Katrusya tied the tree to their sled. Together they pulled the tree home.

"You found a good tree!" the others agreed. Father nailed boards to the bottom of the tree so it would stand erect. Anna and Grandmother filled the washtub with water so the tree would remain fresh and green.

"Welcome, tree! Thank you for bringing Christmas to our house."

"The tree is glad," Katrusya said. "I know."

Anna went through Grandmother's button box. She polished old brass buttons to make them shine, then tied them to the tree as ornaments. Katrusya made a paper star to set at the very top. Ivan and Danilo wove pine boughs into wreaths. Grandfather whittled animals, shepherds, Wise Men, and the Holy Family. Grandmother placed an embroidered cloth in the manger. "This will be a blanket for the Christ Child," she said.

Father began practicing his bandura. "It's been almost a year since I've played Christmas songs. I fear my fingers have forgotten how to play."

"We'll all sing loud," Katrusya insisted. "No one will hear your mistakes."

Mother began baking a *kolach*, the braided Christmas bread. "The hens have been laying well. I think we can spare a little flour and sugar for something special."

That night, Katrusya lay fast asleep when she heard screaming. The whole family ran to see what was wrong.

Mother stood by the stove, pointing her finger at the Christmas tree. "Take it out of my house!"

"What's wrong with the tree?" Katrusya, Ivan, and Danilo asked all at once.

"Take a good look!" Mother said.

Katrusya's heart sank. A tiny brown dot moved across a pine needle. A baby spider! Katrusya counted one, then another, and another.

"There must be hundreds of them!" Danilo exclaimed.

"The mother spiders laid their eggs in the tree at summer's end," said Anna. "The eggs are supposed to hatch when spring comes. When we brought the tree inside the warmth made the spiders hatch. Now they're hungry. They're spinning their little webs among the pine needles."

Sure enough, Katrusya and her brothers saw the tiny silk threads, finer than a baby's hair. Each rippled like liquid silver.

"I won't have spiders in my house!" Mother insisted.

"I'll take the tree outside," said Grandfather.

"No!" the children cried. "Not after we worked so hard to make the tree beautiful."

"Please, Mamaniu!" Katrusya begged. "These baby spiders are so small and helpless. If we take them outside, they'll die in the cold. Let them stay until Christmas is over."

Mother's face softened.

"It won't seem like Christmas without a tree," Grandmother added.

"I suppose I can put up with a few spiders until Christmas is over," Mother agreed at last.

Katrusya threw her arms around Mother's waist. "This is the best Christmas present we could ever have."

The family spent the rest of the day preparing for the Christmas feast. Grandmother spread two embroidered cloths on the table. "One is for the members of our family who are still living," she explained. "The other is for those who have passed on. Their memory is still with us."

"I know," said Ivan. "That's why we set an extra place at the table. And why we put a sheaf of wheat before our family icons. To welcome our whole family, living and dead, into our home on Christmas Eve."

Mother placed the *kolach* in the middle of the table. "Who knows what the Christmas loaf means?"

Danilo answered. "The three rings of bread stand for the Trinity: the Father, the Son, and the Holy Spirit. The circle is a symbol of Eternity. The candle stands for hope and eternal life."

"Very good!" said Grandfather, coming in from the barn. He spread an armload of hay beneath the table. "What about this hay?"

"The hay reminds us that Jesus was born in a barn and laid in a manger," Katrusya said.

The Christmas celebration began when the first star appeared in the sky.

"Times may be hard," said Mother, "but this night we will feast." They sat down to dinner, beginning with *kutia*, porridge mixed with poppy seeds and honey, and ending hours later with *uzvar*, a dessert of twelve different stewed fruits. In between were beet soup, two kinds of dumplings, stuffed cabbage, and fish served six different ways. Katrusya ate so much she felt as stuffed as one of Grandmother's dumplings.

Afterward, the family joined their neighbors at church. Father Roman read from the Bible. The choir sang. So much food made Katrusya sleepy, but she kept herself awake until the end.

"*Khrystos Razhdaietsia!*" Father Roman proclaimed. "Christ is born!"

Father led the family home. As he opened the door, the lantern light cast shadows on the walls.

"The tree! Look at it!" Danilo cried. Tiny spider webs covered the branches from top to bottom.

"They shine like silver!" Anna exclaimed.

"We almost didn't have a Christmas tree. Now we have the most beautiful tree of all," said Grandmother.

"I'm glad we let the spiders stay," Father said.

"So am I," Mother agreed.

Katrusya, entranced, walked up to the tree. She looked for the spiders, but they had all disappeared. She reached out to touch the shining threads.

"Mama! Tato! All of you, come here!" Katrusya cried. These webs feel hard, like wire! Could they have become . . ."

"Silver!" Grandfather touched the web. "They are real silver!"

"And look at the buttons! And Katrusya's star!"

The whole village came running to see the miracle. The spiderwebs that covered the Christmas tree had been magically changed to threads of pure silver. The buttons had become gold coins. And Katrusya's paper star had become a gold and silver spangle covered with jewels.

"It is indeed a miracle," said Father Roman. "You showed kindness to the little spiders by letting them stay in your warm house. In return, the spiders showed thanks by giving you a Christmas present."

"Not just for us!" Katrusya said. "We want to share it with the whole village! *Khrystos Razhdaietsia!* Merry Christmas, everyone!"

And the whole village answered, "*Khrystos Razhdaietsia!* Christ is born! Merry Christmas!"

Author's Note

The story of *The Spider's Christmas* appears in similar versions throughout central and eastern Europe. It has special significance for Ukrainians, who revere the spider as a model of diligence and modesty. Ukrainian Christmas customs are ancient. Their roots lie in the winter solstice celebrations of the earliest Slavic peoples.

The Ukrainian Christmas greeting *"Khrystos Razhdaietsia"* means "Christ is born." People answer, *"Slavimo Ioho,"* meaning "Let us praise him." Another traditional greeting is *"Veselykh Sviat,"* which means "Happy Holidays."